The Berenstain Bears®
VISIT
FARMER BEN

Stan & Jan Berenstain

A GOLDEN BOOK • NEW YORK
Western Publishing Company, Inc., Racine, Wisconsin 53404

We're going to see
our neighbor and friend.
He has a big farm.
It's just 'round the bend.

3

And there's Ben's farm
just up ahead.

As you can see,

it's quite a spread.

5

Where's Farmer Ben?
There he is now.
He's in the barn,
milking a cow.

He's sitting on
his three-legged stool.
He's milking the cow
where it's shady and cool.

The cow says, "Moo!"
Ben's cat says, "Meow!"
and he brushes against
the leg of the cow.

8

The name of Ben's cat
is Mister McBurt.
He wants some milk.
Ben gives him a squirt.

We like Ben's barn.

It's very nice.

Ben's cat likes it, too,

because it has mice.

But, dear friends,
as you can easily see,
Mister McBurt
does not agree.

13

What's that tall thing
right over there?

Why, that's our silo,
Brother Bear.

Here comes my hired bear.

Cubs, meet Mister Milo.

He is the one

who's in charge of the silo.

The silo's the place
where we store the wheat
that we sell to the folks
who make good things to eat.

Because, my friends,
wheat's what it takes

to make the flour

that goes into our bread,

cookies,

and cakes.

17

I have another question, Ben.

Go ahead and ask it, son!

Is farming hard
or is it fun?

Hmm—is farming hard
or is it fun?
Well, it's not a job
for everyone.

There are hogs to slop,

chickens to feed,

fences to fix,

gardens to weed.

There's always our bull
to worry about.

24

We need to be sure
he doesn't get out.

There are sheep to shear.

There's fertilizer to spread.

But when the sun goes down
and the sky is red,
when the livestock are all
bedded down and fed,
and I sit on the porch
with Mrs. Ben....

Er—what was that question
of yours again?

Oh, yes: Is farming hard
or is it fun?

31

Well, it's hard
but I love it, son!
So I guess you might say
farming's *hard fun.*